An Earth & Evermore Novella

Season of Ziyol

John Consalvo

Contents

1: Winter Upon a Fall

It looms everywhere.
Fall, for all its brilliance, escapes me.
In the modern tongue, they shout for "imminent winter" in
celebration.
And for what they celebrate, it is quite the wonder.
But when an oak's beauty fades, it is another reminder that
the tic tocs are again upon me.
The dreams I once had:
All of them I truly believed at one point or another.
The truths I once held:
I preached to the world at one point or another.
In those days, looking back – I was right.
Indeed, I was right. I dreamed of family, and friends, and
G-d's perfect will.
I dreamed of song and laughter.
I dreamed of a soulmate.
I dreamed in innocence.
But today – I've grown.
No longer do I take on the childish ways of my former self.
For the potential of Spring has vanished, summer was wasted:
Now I hold onto the fading remnants of fall in desperation.
The winds, blizzards, ice, and bitter cold of Winter engulfs
the fall…
AND comes for us all.
Too proud I am to admit where I've failed.
Too weak I am to confess that I still do.
Too lost I am to return to prior seasons.
Would I not, in my own vanity, remain lost in resentment
while guiding others to a misplaced path despite it all?

Those that offer to love me – I reject and push away.
Because I know better.
Those who offer me a hand in friendship – I allow my own
circumstances to excuse spending time away from them.
Because I know better.
Those who offer me a drink when thirsty – I decline charity.
Again, I know better.
Oh, how I can hear that lady of the modern tongue use her
words on me saying, "You know nothing!"
And she'd be right.
Except for this one thing:
I hear a still small voice – the one from springs past – deep
within me;
Saying these words over and over:
"Endure and be found, endure and be found, endure and
be found."
What if I fail? "Endure and be found."
What if I struggle? "Endure and be found."
What if I face unforgiveness? "Endure and be found."
And If I am unforgiving? "Endure and be found."
Endure for how long? Found where? By Whom?
"Endure through the winds and storms of Winter's harshness.
You will be saved and found in the land of Spring.
For Spring returns to conquer ALL - even the Winter.
Don't allow its love to pass or be taken for granted.
In doing so, you will be stuck in Winter forever.
Accept Spring's love, and it will melt the wretched ice - for
eternities on end."
The sun rises.

2: Vulnerabilitudes

Shy
Transparent
Hungry
Declarant
Remorseful
Regret it
Unspiteful
Forget it
Exciting
I swear it
Infighting
I wear it
Like lightning
And thunder
I'm frighteningly
Crushed under
Second pause
I feel it
Heart stopping 'cause
She steals it
A decade passes
Train's leaving
Carrying the masses
Deceiving
Wait for me, please
Is it too late?
Hand me the keys
Don't hesitate
Won't this time

To be sure
I've lived like a mime
Now no more
Round and round
And round I stand
In a new place
In a new land
The years move forward
But backwards I go
"On trial for being a dwarf."
And I must let go
In isolation
My own throne
The corrosive lore
of being alone
Where do I go next?
What could I sing?
As I wait this Winter out
Anticipating Spring.

3: The Lions Approach

Can you hear the sound?
Like an icepick chipping away at an old block.
My chattering teeth chant loudly through the forest.
Can you feel the chill from the wind;
bearing down on my cheeks like Christmases past?
In those days, it was sincere to find a gift.
Just the one gift.
Now there is no one left to gather salt for gifts.
Who would receive one from me?
Who would find this bitter cold comforting with me?
The candles are flickering out – one by one.
This old broken-down barn can't hold back the storm.
The pounding of hail and ice is destroying the rooftop.
This place is long abandoned and outdated.
My own body heat is all I have to bring me warmth.
That, and my all-consumed mind of memory and wonder.
The cold soothes my wounds but doesn't remove them.
Orcs from the night continue to feed on pieces of me;
and I fear this barn won't shelter me much longer.
Seven candles were burning; now the seventh has gone out.
Frozen, my legs are.
Hindered from walking, I am.
But I can pull myself towards the nearest window.
Trying to keep quiet and unheard, unseen by orcs.
Looking out over the windowsill, a silhouette is formed.
One displaying her beauty.
Shadows establish her long dark hair.
A majestic gown from impetuous snow.
If my legs could move, I would ask her to dance.

The wind stops.
She is gone.
But not my memory.
From all the daughters of Eve until this moment, none were
more stunning than she.
Even now, during hallucinations in these dark days;
that distant memory brings me hope.
Don't ask why.
I wouldn't know.
I eat, I'm still ravenous.
I thirst, even though I drink.
Where is my purpose?
"You won't like the answer."
The creaking walls tell me.
Part of me wants to give up.
Part of me wants to endure.
I must endure.
My plans have rotted.
At least that's what the wind says.
But even now, I imagine what a moment would be in
that dance.
With her, in a garden of delphiniums.
Therefore, hope is dangerous.
For it is cold, and there are no signs of the orcs subsiding.
What is that?
That sound?
A groan? More like a roar!
The clouds open.
Majestically,
the Lions approach.
Spring is on its way.

4: Stare at Midday

Ferocious, they look in the gleaming sunlight.
Twins with identical manes standing side by side on the hilltop.
They must be here to rescue me from the orc-driven Winter.
The growl and roar from their lungs form a powerful wind through all the land.
Singing birds return to fly around them.
In the surround of each paw, violets and roses appear in all colors.
Truly, Spring is coming with might and magnificence.
I can't help but smile.
I can't help but dream of my hopes again with hope.
That dangerous hope doesn't seem so dangerous now.
In joy, I attempt to leap and run towards our newest guests.
But my legs…Yes, my legs are still frozen from the storm.
Help! I yell towards the great beasts.
Yet, they stay in place without looking in my direction.
Hahahahahahahahahaha.
The orcs laugh and sing,
"Who do you cry 'help' to?"
Was I seeing things?
I'm outside the barn now, trying to pull myself closer yet still so far.
The light over the hill is brilliantly bright.
The clouds overhead turn dark as sackcloth.
"Who do you cry for, human?" the orcs mock me.
I remained silent, now somewhat confused.
"Why cry for those who aren't there? There are none to help you!"
More encouragement from the orcs.
Perhaps hallucinations are again kicking in.
But I can feel the sun in the distance.
And the squint in my eyes is quite real from its glorious shine.

Nipping at my heels, the orcs continue.
Unlike yesterday, they are not surrounding me - but
behind me.
They seem weaker, a little, today.
Maybe it's because of the new light - there is a flame, ever
small, within me.
Burning with desire to fight.
To fight for my survival.
To fight for my name.
To fight for my hopes.
To fight for my dream.
To fight for my life.
To fight for my king.
To fight for my purpose.
And the songs that I sing!
Kicking against their heads;
I do with all my might.
I kick with my toes, opened from broken boots.
I kick with my heels.
I kick them in their eyes.
I kick them in the head.
I kick until they let me go.
I pull myself farther from them.
Slowly they attempt to attack my heels again.
I kick them and pull myself farther from them - closer to
the lions.
"Why pull yourself so far from the barn? Far from where it's
safe?" an orc asked.
I continue the routine.
Kick and pull, Kick and pull.
I look up after hours and hours of kicking and pulling.
The lions are still there!

In the midday air.
Looking past me.
With a midday stare.

5: Princess Audience

Drag me this last mile.
Drag me through the snow and mud and blood of orcs and
my own.
Unable to move under my own power.
Fires up ahead fighting Winter.
"Almost there, almost there," Favri sings.
Almost where? I wonder.
*Something familiar about this Orc, I know his name but cannot
recall how.*
The joy I felt for a mere moment is as far from me as
the lions.
The silhouette of the dancer now a long-lost memory.
"Almost there, hold on, just a little longer," Favri sings,
dragging me towards the fires.
"Hurry, we must-we must." He whispers.
There's a new barn up ahead.
Much like the one I was hiding in earlier.
Yet, this one is unspoiled.
Whereas mine was war-torn.
What have I now to atone for?
I should have stayed on the path towards Spring.
Memories begin to flood my mind as he sings of a princess in
need of a rescue.
Sorrow creeps in.
I am far from my path.
"Her chambers are ahead, friend, in the barn."
I pictured her surrounded by orcs.
Yet, all is quiet around the barn.
As I once was deceiving in life, have I now been deceived?

All that I gave half my heart to, is payment now rendered
to me?
Not even half my heart-I barely gave any of it.
"Look, friend, the door opens."
Indeed, it opens; still, no orcs around.
The door creeks closed behind us.
It's warm in here.
I hate being here.
Yet I am out of the cold.
"Stay put," Favri whispers.
My eyes are blurry.
As curious as I am, I need to sleep.
I need to sleep.
I sleep, and I dream.
I dream, and I sleep.
Lions and the silhouette comfort me.
"Wake!"
"Wake!"
"WAKE!"
My eyes opened.
A massive dark red monster stands over me.
Ferocious.
"Dare you sleep in the presence of the Princess?"
Laughter upon laughter fills the room.
Unless my eyes are lying, I am surrounded by orcs.
Hundreds of orcs.
Even those that attacked my heels prior.
"Humble yourself before her!"
My legs, I can move them.
I can stand.
I can stand.
Yet, I am pushed down.

"Humble yourself!" the large orc shouts.
"You are in the presence of Princess Audience! The ruler of Orctic!"
I am afraid.
Indeed, I made the wrong choice.
Upon hearing her voice and feeling her presence,
I am intrigued.
"Trabble, help our guest to stand," she says softly.
"Have I not worn my hair as emerald green, long as the vines
of Moxawalls?-
Is my gown not shining with splendors of silver and glass?"
The orcs grumble among themselves in agreement.
"Then help our guest to rise!" she demands.
"For he is home."
Home?
Home?
Found and yet more lost I am.

6: The Undertaking

"Hear Ye, Hear Ye!"
The tall, lean yellow orc proclaimed.
"From the Ice lands to the Sand seas,
The daughter of law, sister of might,
Her Majesty, Prince Audience rules the night."
Orcs of all colors, fangs, and sizes cheered her name.
"Aud, Aud, Aud Aud!"
"The destined will be overthrown
Their weakness exposed
While the world witnesses her dynasty
Recreating destinies unopposed.
May every dove run and every raven sing,
The song of her victories
And death to an untrue king."
Shouting and screaming and overjoyed sounds,
ring through my ears and mind.
I could not perceive.
I could not forget.
The feeling of good diminishing within,
quickly replaced with regret.
Deceived I've been.
"But have I deceived you?"
Favri asks while slapping his brown claw on my shoulder.
"Perhaps it's too much ale. You seem of gloom."
How, I wonder, can he express such joy after robbing me of hope?
"Did I not say the Princess would be surrounded by the vilest of orcs?
Did I not say even those who were nipping at your heels?
And here they are!
Did I not say that she desperately needed your help?

Yes, she does.
For our enemies are pounding at the gates,
Ready to undo our own hopes and dreams."
No enemy I have seen.
The armies are drunk, unready for battle.
What is the danger he speaks of?
"You can't feel its power draining on us, but I do."
Favri whispers.
"The cold fires are dying.
The Frozen Roses have withered,
with it, her soon destruction.
No, we don't speak of it to the others.
But rest assured, death comes for us.
We must turn it back."
I'm not sure.
He is either truly friendly, naïve, or simply clever.
The orcs that bloodied me are here.
Yet, they have not come against me at all during my stay.
"Are there no bad humans?" he asked.
"Or dogs, or relatives? We all have that crazy uncle, don't we?
Should we not be accepting or forgiving of our differences?"
This is different.
To me, it's personal.
They attacked me.
Worse, I allowed my dreams, my one chance
at living life to the fullest to be swept away.
"While you wallow in pitying yourself,
Look at where you are now.
The Princess of a great nation adores you at first sight.
You were muddy and bloody when I found you!
Tell me if I speak untruths!
You could not walk.

You could barely crawl
And your crawl was towards whims, dreams,
and hallucinations.
I risked my very life to get you.
In doing so, I brought you to safety.
Your selfishness blinds you from this."
I'm blinded – indeed I am.

7: Raider Entrant

A new day it is.

My eyes are open, body warmed by the fire.

Even so, there are chills within.

My bed, soft as feathers with blankets of thick black fur.

I believe a bear donated his pelt for such comfort.

Favri was right; my legs are better.

And yes, it's certainly warmer in here than out there.

Still, my heart longs for Spring.

BOOM!

My door has been kicked in!

There is smoke everywhere!

The top of my gown nearly ripped off me.

I'm thrown down to the floor.

"Why are you here?"

A female sounding being looking much like an orc asks.

Her left knee presses strong between my throat and chest.

Her silver hair shines beautifully near the fire.

But there are daggers in her eyes.

Anger is written on her face.

"What do you hear?"

She asked me angrily.

Her right claw covers my mouth to keep me from answering.

"You are NOT supposed to be here!" she utters.

Finally, someone is making sense.

"How am I supposed to not kill you when the time comes?"

Okay, perhaps she isn't making sense.

"Are you not to wed the Princess?"

Wed? That better not mean what I think it means.

"The newcomer! The newcomer! The Princess and
the newcomer!
It's all they are saying now!" the intruder murmurs.
My heart is pounding, and my head shakes in the negative.
Hoping beyond all hope that she is wrong.
It's about as comforting as being brought here as an entrée.
I'm still not convinced that I haven't been.
Quickly, trying to gather my wits.
Can't help but notice-
actual daggers all around her belt,
which causes me further panic.
All I can see are the glass handles.
Quite intimidating.
Her smooth, obsidian face has smaller fangs-
than the others.
I struggle to speak.
"SHH! Can you hear that?"
I hear nothing.
Her eyes widen.
She is hearing something.
Voices in her head, perhaps.
Great, just great. As if things couldn't get worse.
Now I have a psychotic captor.
BAM!
With one lightning-fast flick of her wrist,
She unleashed one of her daggers towards a wall opposite
the fireplace.
"I knew it!"
Squinting my eyes.
To get a better look.
Focusing – did she hit anything?

Another dagger comes out towards a different part of
the wall.
BAM!
And another!
BAM!
Now several towards the ceiling.
BAM! BAM! BAM!
What is happening?
She finally stops and gently lifts her knee from my chest.
I am trained well not to make a sound.
Over to the wall, she goes and grabs the first dagger.
I can see a green mist.
She peels something off the wall and brings it to me.
It's a spider-or was a spider.
Eight legs with black and brown fur.
And yes, green blood.
"They are watching you!" she whispered.
"Always watching you they are."
Interestingly,
my door is still in place.

8: Laureate Roundabout

The door swings open.
"Hear Ye, Newcomer!" said the tall thin yellow orc.
"It seems an intrusion has taken place,
Without the permission of Her Grace.
The Raider Entrant in this room,
Uses trickery to build your doom.
If she's asked, she will deny.
Trials won't work here, that is why.
I'll spread gossip to the court instead.
Thus, public opinion will snare her head.
It may be harsh; it may be quick,
It may be troubling; it may be sick.
What you call twisted, I call fate.
You say 'lies,' I say 'fabricate.'
All in all, it's in good fun.
To keep the Princess from this one.
Fellow orcs gather round,
And force this Raider to be bound.
Newcomer, keep your distance from her, please.
She is viler than the worst disease.
Time to go, orcs, don't hesitate.
Kill off this disgrace for spewing her hate."
The poet and his fellow lookalike orcs
carried the Raider away.
They chanted the next day's headlines:
"Raider Traitor! Raider Traitor!"
Like a wildfire, the chants go from the small circle of
poet orcs
to the others.

Even the childlike orcs laugh and shout the headline.
"Are you safe, my friend?" Favri asks in a panic upon visiting.
"Quite frightened I was when I heard the Raider
attacked you."
Was I attacked?
"Conniving those Raiders are. They break in, throw you
down, and show off those daggers!
I'm glad the Poet Police were here in time.
Nothing gets past them, you see? Nothing at all!"
How did he find out so quickly?
I wonder.
"If you are wondering how I knew of your incident,
Well, it's all over town.
By the sounds of it, the poets got the votes."
Got the votes?
"Newcomer, listen to them! Those boisterous Raider
Traitor shouts.
Coming from everywhere!
By Farrah's Fangs, I'd be shocked if that filthy Raider wasn't
executed today!
It's what the public wants."
Is anyone going to question me?
I mean, I was there.
"What is so prodigious about this system, Newcomer, is
everyone gets what they want.
No more raiders breaking in, no more daggers on the loose,
no more lies being spread."
What lies were spread?
"Anything she said – had to be a lie. See? There's the proof.
The green mist on the wall!"
The spider blood?
"She probably told you it was spider blood.

Making you think it was an infestation.
Rest assured, my friend, no spiders live here. They were
planted.
You were about to be deceived."
By now, Favri's face is noticeably different.
Is he frightened, concerned, or delighted?
By all accounts, the morning has been strange already.
It's about to get stranger.
"My Prince, My Prince!"
Princess Aud pushes her way through.
"Did they hurt you? You must have been terrified?
I would have been?"
Does it even matter if I answer at this point?
Amidst the chaos, I can't help but notice
The Princess has changed from all greens into shades
of pinks.
For an orc, she looks very pretty.
"I just knew you would like me in these colors. Favri wasn't
quite sure, but I knew my Prince."
She kisses me on the cheek.
Favri shrugs his shoulders.
I'm guessing that means' go with it?'
"I will have them execute her at once!" Princess Aud said.
Motioning to her entourage of orc soldiers.
"No one does this to my Prince."
Since when did I become her Prince?
I feel like a prisoner.
"The people want the Raider eliminated, and so do I!
Kooples – have your Orchenches readied!
It has been a long time coming for that one."
Kooples, the head guard, bowed his head in affirmation.
The Princess and the entourage left.

Favri closes the door behind them.

"I meant to tell you about this wedding idea.

Mere rumor, actually.

But- before it was front-page news...."

What wedding?

What is happening?

Why are the guards binding my hands?

Where are they taking me?

Why was I attacked?

Favri? Favri is gone. How did he disappear?

Lightheaded.

Dizzy.

Yet awake.

When will the nightmare end?

How I long for Spring.

9: The Proposal

"I asked you to the throne room for a specific purpose,"
said the seated Princess,
within an emptied echo-filled hall.
"Favri has let me know of your concerns,
regarding the criminal – that Raider."
Favri is quite perceptive, come to think of it.
I don't recall *actually* telling him.
Nonetheless, Favri is correct.
"He says, you feel we might be dealing with our guest
somewhat harshly?"
Several of the Princess' guard slowly entered the shadow-
ridden chamber.
Impossible to ponder the sum of nerves jittering within me.
How should I respond?
"Whatever your feelings, my Prince, I must inform you,
we deal hastily with criminals in our lands.
With good reason.
Several centuries ago, these Raiders,
Like the one who attacked you,
treated us quite poorly.
They were massively wealthy.
These lands were filled with castles.
Overflowing, producing areas of fruit and tree and flower.
Raiders, in their beauty and wealth, took us for granted.
The lowly of us, the oppressed, who weren't as beautiful as they,
were not invited to their world.
We weren't even outcasts –just non-existent.
**We toiled the land, we did the work, and they reaped
the reward.**
Over time, we eroded that society.

Eventually, I was chosen as Princess over all orc lands.
My pledge to our people was simple:
We would cease to non-exist.
Never again would we be an afterthought.
Now, look at us.
No, we cannot match their obsidian beauty.
No, the lands are not producing what they once did.
While true, the castles that formerly stood in glory are now
reduced to barns,
we have forced those who oppressed us to feel what we
once felt.
In this, there is justification.
In this, there is honor.
In this, there is retribution.
Never again will the raiders be allowed to roam these
lands freely.
I don't imprison her just because she attacked you.
I know deep down we truly imprison her because,
of her beautiful skin, because of our history,
because she is a Raider, and Raiders are all the same."
Absorbing her words, my spirit is troubled.
Her guards pound the ground with spears in agreeance.
The pain and anguish from her words fill the room.
It's hard to imagine these lands were once flourishing
and beautiful.
It's always Winter.
"Knowing all of this, what would you have me do,
my Prince?"
Princess Aud's eyes were directly upon me.
That same pink doe-like glance,
Aimed towards me earlier in the day,
now replaced with a fierce wine-colored,

look of determination.
I guess it is my turn to respond.
I am petrified of her guards,
who look ready to add me to the lunch menu.
I lift my right hand and begin to speak.
"Excuse me, your majesty," Favri interrupted.
Slowly he emerges from the shadows.
I hadn't noticed him, has he been here the whole time?
Who else is in the shadows? I wonder.
"Perhaps, a proposal to consider?" Favri approached
the throne.
His light brown claw handed over a scroll.
"This is an old seal from 400 years ago, Favri."
She frowns.
"And it's been opened."
"By many leaders before you, Your Grace," Favri interjected.
"Humbly, I ask you to read the ancient text."
Princess Audience opens the scroll.
I wonder why Favri chose this moment to interrupt
the Princess.
I'm trying to study her face.
Stoic, she is, like an uncut stone.
Impossible to get a glimpse at her thoughts.
"Your majesty," Princess Audience reads aloud.
"Whether or not this post reaches you is beyond my eyes.
I am King Chief Ruler Boltokanz of the fanged nations.
The fanged nations of beast, orc, and Raider kind alike.
I, myself, am of the Raider lands.
Fear has obsessed my heart.
My kin have embraced ignorance, I'm afraid.
They wake up, do their work, and enjoy the riches of the day.
In doing so,

there are those who are unable to do as such.
Those that are ignored.
Thus, the seeds of hatred and resentment fester.
By the time you receive this some years from now,
The Raider ruling family will have long been removed from
the throne.
I am writing to you because I am dying.
I have made a grave error in judgment.
An orc was brought before the throne.
Accused of stealing food for his family.
Rightly, according to our laws, I caged him.
Years passed.
Evidence mounted that another orc, a different orc called
Amoy,
was the true thief.
I did not ask for help on the case, or evidence, or a trial.
I asked the public.
Amoy was a cunning orc. He sang great songs.
Spoke words that made our fanged nation feel good.
Because of this, they chose Amoy's side.
In order to gain their favor, I chose incorrectly.
Wipple, the orc imprisoned wrongly, remained imprisoned.
After the trial, while Wipple slept,
One of Amoy's fanged guards killed him in his sleep.
Amoy gathered all of the fanged nations together for a great
feast the next morning.
Around his neck, he wore Wipple's claws and fangs as a
necklace,
Wipple's eyes pierced his ears as jewelry.
His carcass was divided into the main course of Amoy's feast.
At its end, when all the masses were drunk and celebrating the
great day,

Amoy announced the slaying of Wipple.
He showed off Wipples Fangs, Claws, and Eyes to the masses.
Then he shared that Wipple's remains were in all their bellies.
In their stunned silence, they listened intently for Amoy's
next words.
He admitted to his thievery.
Said it was because of successful orcs like Wipple that he
needed to steal.
He accused Wipple, an orc of his own kind, of being an
oppressor and full of greed.
Amoy was far wealthier than the hardworking Wipple.
His words seduced the fanged nations.
They cheered him and cheered him more.
Violence and destruction of our beautiful cities had begun.
All celebrated poor Wipple's demise.
His she-orc was burned alive, and their offspring melted
into jewels.
No longer do I sleep.
The hunger is never quenched with food nor my thirst
with water.
I beg you to look upon my mistake as a mistake,
and learn from it.
May no other suffer from the same callous decisions I made.
I ask you to be bigger than I was and look beyond my blindness
and our ignorance.
A leader leads with conscience,
and should not be driven by what is popular.
For what is popular in one day may be wrong for all following
generations.
I failed here.
Whoever you are, when reading this, you have a chance to
change course,

toward a brighter future.
A future that removes the squabbles amongst us and
unites the fanged nations against the common enemy.
The REAL enemy. Ziyol."
The scroll rolled together and bounced slightly off the floor
where Princess Audience dropped it.
"No one pick it up!" she demanded.
"What should I do, my Prince?
Should I follow the words of an ancient enemy Raider king?
Should I heed the calls of the poets and my fellow orcs?
Should I cast my vision forward and promise like so many
others to restore orc glory?
Should I just do…nothing?
What say you, my Prince?"
"Perhaps…" Favri again interjected.
"We could allow the young prince to examine her
for himself?"
"No!" The Princess responded defiantly.
"It's forbidden!"
Favri, with his head bowed, approached the Princess again
and humbled his body lower.
"By law, yes…But YOU are the Princess Audience. The
rightful ruler of all Orclands.
 It is said that all for a Millennia will worship your name.
Are you bound by such things as laws written by others, even
our enemies?"
Calmly, her face stoic as before, she retorted.
"But the people. They want the Raider executed."
It was unclear if she was taking Favri's counsel to heart.
"Your majesty, imagine the poets reciting the new visionary
rule of their Princess-
and her new Prince."
Favri winked at me.

"You think they will—" she asked.

"I think," Favri lifted his body and took a step up to the same level as the throne.

"I think the orcs are ready for their passions to be stoked by something new."

"Very well. I will do one better, Favri!" The Princess stood.

"I will free her."

The room immediately murmured.

Favri clearly was curious, if not concerned.

"Well, What—" Favri was interrupted.

"I will free her. On one condition." The princess said loudly.

She then looked at me.

"The future Prince accepts this as his wedding gift."

Again, this wedding idea. I do not want to marry Audience or any other orc.

"As my husband and Prince, he will retain authority over a piece of the Orclands.

Forever bound to Winter's realm may he be. Forever bound, a Prince."

I feel sick at the thought.

The silhouette of my dreams is my heart's desire.

Murmuring is louder.

Wedding gift?

"If there is a wedding today between the Newcomer and me, then I will free her, yes, the Raider girl.

I, Audience, the true ruler of the fanged nations, will show mercy.

If not, then she will face the current laws of the orc.

Death by feeding.

This is my proposal!"

So saith the Princess.

10: Ceremony

Six years.
Six long years have passed since the ceremony.
On a rooftop, I sit embracing Winter's call;
while looking across the seas towards Summer worlds.
Each day passes.
I am filled more and more with regret.
How could I have allowed my destiny to be swallowed up?
Dreams of the silhouette persist, but I know time has passed.
There is no road that leads me to Spring now.
What choice did I have?
Would they not have killed the Raider?
I keep telling myself this.
Deep inside, I wish I mustered up the backbone to
fight regardless.
Maybe I would have lost.
Or maybe I would be in Spring now.
My body is numb to the snow and ice.
I remember they had her…
The Raider girl,
in a noose awaiting my appearance for the ceremony.
I was heartbroken.
What kind of beings was I marrying into?
This wasn't who I wanted to marry.
But in my attempts to survive, I went along with it.
I've learned just going along with it,
minimizes everything.
There were no vows spoken.
Drops of my blood were mixed with drops of Princess
Audience's blood

as the orcs chanted:
"Prince to slave, slave to Prince!"
Blood was put in a cauldron and mixed by the Elder Orc
Priestess, Gelhar.
I recall she was the tallest orc in the room.
Gelhar wore an extremely long, sleeveless grey gown.
She spoke strange words over the blood.
Charged us to each drink of the mix.
They chanted some more.
Every orc was there.
Hundreds, thousands
all crammed into this large barn.
At this moment, I had my last chance to say, "No!"
My spine curled like that scroll.
I said nothing and drank the mix.
I drank my dreams, hopes, destinies, and life away.
That feeling of my soul slipping absent, harrowing,
still haunts me.
All I remember beyond that was waking up the next morning.
How troubled my insides were.
Waking up next to an orc bride,
without an ounce of joy or peace to show for it.
My family would be distraught to no end.
The war took them all.
Such are the small wins at this juncture.
"We did it!" I recall her saying,
Next to me with the biggest fanged smile.
We barely knew one another.
She said it as if it was a lifelong effort.
"I honestly never thought we would. I thought you would
back out."

Hearing her say this so nonchalantly made me sick.
Knowing my dreams of the silhouette were just that.
I tried to convince myself this was real love.
But it wasn't love at all.
What I felt and feel for the silhouette
Is love in abundance.
My family would tell me to move on with my life and
embrace this.
Even though they wouldn't approve of the people I've
marrying into now.
Six years later, thinking of those thoughts.
Still, if I could talk to that person,
The person I was,
I'd try convincing him he had a chance to escape.
But now…I don't see a way.
In six years, she's had six orc children.
None are mine.
I'm calling that a small win.
Her children are dreadful creatures.
They are raised to bring chaos, spite, and envy into
every situation.
It goes without saying; they hate me.
The Princess tells them of the outsider I was.
How I was forced to marry.
She tells them of the many husbands she's taken,
and she keeps for her own.
All those orcs cheering at the ceremony,
thinking back, she had wedded.
I sit on this rooftop, not for a hobby,
but these are my quarters.
I am under guard constantly.

I sacrificed my future for no future.
I gave my innocence to no bride.
All I have now is hope to wake up.
Not even dangerous hope –just dead hope.
Favri, ever the friendly orc, visits daily.
I am a Prince in Orcland, after all.
The official title is Prince of the Rooftop.
The guards watching me are supposed to be for
my protection.
They stand silently.
Only grumble when I move across the rooftop.
My conscience was right.
"Friend, what news from the great rooftop?"
Favri asked after climbing up.
He tosses me a rotted pear to eat.
The one chance a day for a meal.
"Still fantasizing about other worlds?
You know it really isn't so bad.
A Prince has perks.
I should have told you she takes most of the males
as husbands.
But our laws forbid such secrets to newcomers.
And look at you now.
I can share secrets with you because you are no longer
a newcomer.
You, my friend, are Prince of the Rooftop Realm.
Quite the ring to it if you ask me."
The pear is as rotted on the inside as the outside.
Perhaps I could negotiate some birds to find me a worm
or two.
"I know you are upset," Favri continued.
"All is not lost.

As the sole brother of Her Grace, I do have some sway with
the guards.
How would you like a walk?
We could retrace our steps from the beginning.
You were such a fool for visions and shadows then.
From my perspective, you are better for coming here,
than dreaming there.
You are only six years into your new destiny.
Lives in the Orcland are eternal.
Another secret I can bestow."

11: Black Myst

"As I said, the guard can easily be persuaded."
Favri boasts.
From the start, Favri's accent reminded me of a buddy
from school.
His family was from France, which stood out in
our neighborhood.
I wonder if there are any orcs from France.
"It has snowed quite muchly since we passed this way six
years back.
You had no strength in your legs.
Look at you now."
As usual, Favri feels the need to remind me how he helped me
to walk again.
I think I will stumble around a bit to humble him.
"I know you must be angry.
Your wife is with another, and life hasn't panned out as
you hoped.
I understand quite well." Favri nodded as we trudged through
the snow.
I didn't feel cold.
Walking around freely again reminds me of summers on
the boardwalk.
The wind picks up, and my skin is also immune to cold.
Nearly seven years in Winter,
most spent on a rooftop will do that to a person.
"You know it's your fault," Favri charged.
My fault?
"Your life. It would have turned out much better
had you made better choices.
When I found you, you had already delved into Winter.

If you wanted to be in Spring
with the lions and that silhouette you dream of,
then why didn't you delve into Spring?
What made you choose Winter?
I certainly didn't."
Favri is right.
I torment myself with these questions hundreds of times
each day.
I'm sure I was afraid or nervous or thought I had more time.
But the harshness of my choices is real
and those dreams are dead!
"Nonetheless," he said, "this life could be a good one.
We have many Princes and chiefs and those with power to
rule the air.
And…
Should you choose to make your stay here,
your position will be eternal,
with the potential to grow great in the kingdom."
Grow great? I get to be Prince of two rooftops then?
"Stop." Favri barred his arm across my chest.
"Something approaches."
He slowly stepped forward in his normal hunched frame.
In all these years,
this is the first time I didn't see a hint of confidence.
"We should turn back." He whispered.
"At once!"
Favri clearly was startled. His fangs are chattering.
And not from the cold.
Trouble clearly is on the brink.
He turns around to head back to the Orclands.
Before joining him, I look ahead, seeing only snow
Shifting back and forth within heavy winter winds.

"AHHHHHHHHHHHHHHH!!!!" Favri screams.

He drops to one knee.

I rush to him.

Breathing but in pain.

"AHHHHHHHHH!!!" Again, he screams, bowing lower towards the snowy surface.

What is happening?

I can't tell if Favri is sick suddenly or wounded somehow.

My questions are answered.

Before another scream from my orc friend,

an ice dagger pierces his forehead,

shattering in one glittering motion.

His breathing stops.

Forgetting about my own safety,

I try to revive him.

Flooding through my mind are memories.

I'd be lost in this place without him.

Favri is my only friend.

I try to press on his chest several times.

No response.

I see no blood or evidence of other punctures.

His body is becoming like rock.

I know life is leaving him,

there is nothing I can do.

Under his eyes, small spots are gathering.

Perhaps it is dirt?

The spots grow larger and cover his face.

It looks like wet soil.

Within seconds his entire body is covered.

"Get away!"

A new voice.

A female voice.

"Get away quick!"
From out of the windy snow,
There she is!
The Raider from six years ago.
The one who attacked me,
Who I ultimately freed.
"If the myst gets on you, death will follow," she said.
She looked the same as she did six years ago.
Why is she doing this to me?
I freed her. I showed her kindness.
The one friend I had in this place,
She has now taken from me.
"We are even, Newcomer."
She said while mending the shattered daggers from
Favri's body.
"You should go.
You have ventured into Raider lands.
Great danger is near.
Do not go from whence you came.
Do not go to where you are going.
Do not stay here.
Leave and leave quickly."
Just as she arrived, she vanished through the snow.
I can't go forwards or backwards or stay here.
What do I do?
It's all happening so fast. I don't know what to do.
I'm cracking fast. I can't breathe.
I can't breathe.
My right hand. It burns.
Opening my fists which had been clenched this whole time.
I find…
Black Myst.

12: My Own Understanding

Where am I?
In foreign Raider territories?
Favri is not here to guide me,
The Black Myst has gripped me.
It is dark and windy.
Tumultuous snowstorms are everywhere.
I miss my dear Favri.
Maybe he wasn't the closest friend – but in this place…
He was my only friend.
Delirium is setting in.
My senses are slipping away.
Where is my rooftop?
I long for it now.
How foolish of me to leave for dreams of Spring.
Who am I to have the audacity to dream?
Dreams are for great men.
Men born rich, powerful, handsome - yes
Dreams were made for those.
I should have been happy as a Prince of some
random rooftop.
Now I'm more lost than I was before.
I think I see something.
Up ahead.
It looks like a series of flames.
Perhaps I am back in the Orclands.
I couldn't be happier if that were true.
Oh, the irony in that thought.
I'm getting closer.
I see six torches in the snow.

Three on each side as if creating a pathway.
I continue.
What have I to lose?
The flames are brighter; I get closer.
I feel no heat - not that the cold bothers me.
I still feel nothing.
Looking around, I see only torches.
Who put these here?
I see no orcs.
I see no Raiders.
I see no visions of lions or Spring.
Just flames in the darkness, flames in the storm.
Wait!
I'm off balance.
I'm falling and falling fast,
into shadow and still falling.
Still falling!
BAM!
…
…
…
My eyes are half-open.
I'm dizzy.
I'm drowsy.
Have I hit bottom?
In a massive pit or ditch, I'm trapped.
Flat on my back, I see stars overhead,
though the storm persists.
The myst on my right hand is expanding.
I'm grabbing for any snow I can find to soothe it.
I noticed earlier that snow slows the myst.
It only does so much; my right hand is now all black.

The myst is travelling up my arm.
It burns!
I have not the strength to get up.
No choice but to rest here.
"This is where you die!"
I hear a voice say to me.
It's in my head.
Maybe it's true.
Sleep, I need sleep.
No friends, no home,
just isolated and forced to face these truths.
And rest.

13: Pality

The skies are blue.
I hear echoes of wind against the ditch banks.
The storm has passed.
Sleep captivated me in this trench for hours.
The Black Myst hasn't spread beyond the forearm.
As rejuvenated as I feel from the rest,
lingering here doesn't feel like the best plan.
But...
Any effort to lift myself up is futile.
I'm still trapped.
Attempting again to lift my back from the ground,
still, nothing moves.
It's as if I am cemented to this ditch.
Hyperventilation sensors are a go.
Panic mode is quickly setting in.
BOOM!
The ground shakes.
A quake of some kind?
BOOM!
Another tremor - more powerful than the first.
BOOM!
The vibration from this third shake has loosened me.
BOOM! BOOM!
I've not a care for what is causing the tremors-just break
me free.
BOOM! BOOM! BOOM!
This last shake causes rocks and boulders to break all around.
My neck snaps back.
My head grazes one of the falling rocks,

while the quake is lifting me off the ground painfully.
Yes! I am free.
Water is filling the ditch.
I'm doing everything I can to get out of here.
Using the reddish mud as footholds to assist in my
feverish climb.
It's soggy and slippery.
The mud from the climb is mingled with blood and open
wounds from my head.
I'm near the top. It's not as deep as I thought.
Deep, nonetheless.
I'm out.
I CAN BREATHE.
The sudden panic is now in retreat.
On my knees, I fall.
The snow is a blistering white light reflected from the sun
causing blindness to my eyes, but I don't care.
The storm has subsided.
No more daggers, or ditches, or prison-like rooftops.
No more fog and no more wind blowing snow in my face.
Let me absorb this moment of peace.
With my eyes closed, allowing the sun to beat upon my face
is magnificent.
It's the small wins.
It's not the heat but the light I feel.
And now it's fading,
  and fading,
  and gone.
My eyes are opened and adjusted.
The skies are still blue.
But I am covered by a shadow.
BOOM!

Off the ground, I go soaring into the air.
BAM!
I land harshly on an icy snow hill.
Immediate terror fills my soul.
What is before me?
I fear it and don't know of it.
It's large, perhaps sixty feet in height, and almost the same
size in width.
It has a face with fangs and dark blue porcupine-looking
needles for hair.
Its claws alone are at least twice my frame.
It is not breathing through its horseshoe-shaped nose
Or dark wine-colored mouth.
And yet, it's very much alive.
No facial mannerisms or sounds I can hear.
It just stares and stares…at me.
What a Beast!
With its long orangutan-like arm, a swipe comes in
my direction.
In one swoop, I am now in its clutches.
Off the ground, I am lifted in its palm.
We immediately move south.
BOOM! BOOM!
With each step.
The feet of the beast, I can see from up here, are mammoth.
Its footprints cause massive ditches, like the one I was
in, everywhere.
Ironically – I don't fear this beast.
I just want to get somewhere, and it probably knows where
somewhere is.
With each thunderous BOOM, the ground shakes.
The beast is moving at great speed.

In the distance, I see a massive set of wavy vines.
They are black.
The beast is heading there.
Perhaps that is its lair?
The surroundings are unfamiliar to me.
Indeed, this is somewhere new.
In fact, it is somewhere.
With all the bouncing up and down, combined with the grasp
from his claw
nearly suffocating me at this point,
I can't tell, yet it seems as if the wavy vines
are a fortress-
or perhaps a castle of sorts.
I can make out a black wall surrounding it.
The speed of the beast has gotten us here quickly.
AGHHHH!
My head!
Unceremoniously the beast drops me in front of the wall.
Facial wounds the winds cured have been re-opened.
"Well done, Lof," I hear a male voice from behind the wall.
The beast doesn't make a sound or move.
A tall obsidian-colored being with shining silver hair
just floated through the wall towards us.
Okay, how bad is this bump on my head?
He looks like the Raider that attacked me,
except for the red ears and chin.
"Lof, you have brought us a prize, have you?"
The being immediately inspects me.
I meant to warn him of the Black Myst but stay silent.
Nonetheless, he examines that area closely.
"You've used the snow to keep the myst from advancing.
He must not know of its power, Lof."

Power? It's going to kill me!
The being waves his long atramentous fingers back and forth.
The walls open.
"Lof, you may feed while I tend to our guest."
Indeed, the wavy vines were not vines but part of a
palatial structure.
A magnificent obsidian shiny structure.
Far from the barn houses in the Orclands.
The beast enters, lifts a massive ground cover, and jumps in.
The cover is back in place.
Instantly, the beast is gone from my sight.
"You, Newcomer, are in the realm of Pality.
I am Ziyol, its Chief Prince."
He motions for me to follow.
The blow to my head has me woozy.
Ziyol waves his hands in circular motions.
A nearby cord flys towards me,
and wraps my head.
Incredibly the vertigo and pain are replaced with tingles.
"Much better, I imagine," he said mockingly.
"I am not the first raider you have seen; I think?"
I subtly shake my head.
"A real raider would not have left you alive
and yet here you are.
Let us sit out in the courtyard.
I cannot kill you now, so if you are wondering about your life,
let me spare you the wasted time on dwelling.
You, Newcomer, bear the mark of the myst.
And those who bear the mark of the myst
are to be treated as equals among us."
Who is us?

* * *

Ziyol's tall, thin frame walks in front of me.
"Follow me, boy!" he mocks.
His silver and black studded coat drags behind in the snow,
in perfect motion with his nonchalant pace.
"Have you learned anything, Newcomer?
I mean, besides having no understanding of that weapon
forming on your arm.
The journey, has it taught you anything?"
I've learned many things.
And many more, I'm sure, if I only had a moment to process.
I stay silent.
"I've watched you, Newcomer.
I watched your struggles leaving Fall then exiled into Winter.
I saw how gullible you were to the seductions in the Orclands.
I snickered at your wasted sacrifice for an unknown killer.
I laughed at your agreeing to marry the Princess Audience
against your own wishes.
I yawned at your playful attempts to win over her children.
And smiled gleefully watching you toil on those rooftops.
BUT!" He yelled while stopping on the top step leading into
the palace.
That long-crooked finger pointed in my direction,
piercing my heart with a burn.
**"BUT I was TRULY entertained watching you begin your
journey to the south world."**
With just a flick of his wrist,
massive black wooden doors open towards us.
"Come, boy, let me show you real purpose and real power."
The haunting doors close behind us.
Immediately I feel as if I am in an old cathedral.

47

There are red and black candles flickering everywhere.
Fangs showing from still gargoyles, statue-like,
are causing my insides to shake.
It is warmer.
I can't tell if it is the dark shadowy nature of the palace,
but the myst has crept further up my arm.
There are humans in prostrated positions throughout the palace.
"They are in deep mediation to the raider gods,"
Ziyol says as he walks past the large foyer
and into a new room.
It is quieter and better lit.
The grey, black, and red walls stretch into a long hallway
with many doors on each side.
"I wonder if you've learned that sacrificing yourself
Is pointless?"
Ziyol's hands clasped behind his back.
"What did you gain by sacrificing your time for Favri,
or your will and desire,
for a murderous raider and the Princess of Orclands?"
The sounds of his questions make me afraid.
Afraid of this place, afraid of him, and afraid he might be right.
"We shall see if you've learned soon enough.
First, show me your hand, the good one."
Instinctively I show my left, but quickly change to the right,
considering that was the hand covered in myst.
 "See? Did you decide to show me the hand with the myst,
or was it my will which caused you to change?"
With ease, he waves his hands over the floor pulling up many of
the wood planks.
With just as much ease, he forms two chairs from the wood and a
large table.
"Come sit, Newcomer. Come see what is south of us."

With the floor gone, I can see everything happening
beneath us.
Humans, by the hundreds and thousands, walking around in
a circle.
Each human taking small pieces of themselves,
And handing their pieces to beings that looked-
just like Lof.
A payment of sorts?
No break in their routine.
One after another in large circles, like zombies,
ripped off pieces of themselves, flesh, bone, and handed
it over.
For every Lof-like creature they passed,
this ritual was performed.
The creatures would feed and grow on the pieces!
"How sheepish humans are, wouldn't ya say?
Look at them. Not a word. They just hand it over.
Even the loyal subjects you saw meditating in the foyer,
they whimper and wallow in silence.
Can you guess what is happening below us, Newcomer?"
It was troubling to me.
I couldn't quite tell, but my spirit was sick inside.
He was right.
None fought or questioned or attempted to run.
They just kept walking around in the same circles.
"Unsurprisingly, you are as loud as they are.
Every human down there has a talent.
A greatness within them that they are meant to use.
But of their own free will,
they hand over the time given to use that talent,
and even the talent itself, bit by bit, to us.
We devour it.

It gives us more power.
The best part is their fellow humans, the ones you saw in
the foyer,
those loyal priests to us, that meditate,
those are the ones who convince them
to hand over the talents.
Eventually, we will feast on the priests as well.
As I said, like sheep.”
My insides shivered.
What is this horror before me?
Nothing like this have I seen in all my days.
The fears felt in the Orclands pale in comparison to this.
“Isn’t it beautiful, Newcomer?
In a different time, in the days of Earth,
Humans are handing over their destinies
in exchange for… temporal riches and social statuses of
the day.
It seems like a one-sided deal when you think about it.
But who am I to challenge their will?”
Ziyol snickered and laughed.
“Stretch your left hand towards the wooden table I created.”
The left? I’m confused. I thought he wanted the myst one.
“Just do as I say. Imagine the table splitting in two.
Are you imagining? Can you see it splitting in your mind?”
I nod.
And nothing happens.
“Now do so again, with your right hand.”
I stretch out my right hand towards the table.
With my eyes closed, I see the table snap in two,
Visualize the splintering shards flying across the room.
“Open your eyes, Newcomer.”
To my shock, the table was split as I imagined it.

"Just a simple taste of REAL power.
And to think, you were trying to cover this up?
Man and beast alike search the worlds on end for this power,
and here it finds you."
I stared at my hand.
More fear comes upon me.
There was also a surge of excitement within me
that I had this - This thing.
"You see down there? That is Lof's brother.
He looks like Lof, doesn't he? He used to abuse Lof when he
was younger.
Now he abuses humans and bullies their dreams away from
them
piece by piece.
Doesn't a beast like that deserve to be slaughtered?
Just think, what kind of slaughtering would Lal, Lof's
brother, deserve?"
Just hearing about the cruelty Lal laid upon others,
and watching with my own eyes,
angered me.
I thought for a moment about the zombie-like humans
devouring him alive.
Just for a brief second, I thought this.
And to my horror-
that's exactly what unfolded before me.
The humans turned from their circle and in unison
gnawed and tore at Lal's flesh with their teeth and fingernails.
They resembled wild beasts, not civilized humans.
I couldn't help but vomit profusely.
How could I have done this?
I got up from my chair and ran away from the floor opening.
To my knees, I fell, covering my eyes, and nothing could fight

the tears falling from my face.
"Why weep, Newcomer?
Lal was cruel in life and deserved such a death.
I think you have judged rightly,"
Ziyol said while motioning the chair back under me.
"Those humans in the circle that attacked him,
they called themselves Khrimsonites in the days of Earth.
It's hard to explain, but while we are here in the
Winter World,
They are still on Earth in their time.
Oblivious to our existence.
They know nothing of the circle they walk in.
And these Khrimsonites, Newcomer, they are vile.
They burn children alive for fun and profit.
Justified by new laws in their day.
Barbaric.
Are you so surprised they would look like animals in
this place?
They abuse children any which way they desire.
And will continue to do so unless dealt with.
Oh, and the security measures of the day,
turn their heads for social status and payment.
Just watch."
In that moment, I saw a vision of children being
skinned alive,
in the presence of these Khrimsonites.
They laughed and trampled the skulls of the little ones.
Well dressed, they were, and respected in society.
No one saw the joy in the horror these Khrimsonites
embraced.
I saw the future. And they kept on doing it, repeatedly
at random.

"Have you ever seen monsters like these, Newcomer?"
Ziyol gently petted my head.
"Surely, you are a righteous and good soul. Surely you are
worthy of passing judgment?"
I couldn't help myself.
For a split second, I thought of those children rising and
slaying each member
of the Khrimsonites.
The next moment,
the gang vanished before my eyes into dust.
Ziyol let out a wicked laugh.
"You are powerful.
Well,
fairly well."

14: Ziyol's Musing

"Freedom is such a fruitless way-wouldn't ya say?"
Ziyol sang upon entering my chambers.
"The sun is out over all the lands, and those dumb souls,
they don't understand.
Nor do they have a say,
in how much longer it shines today.
Close your eyes to wish it Spring?
Sir, do you know anything?
It's morning, yes, but what do ya know?
The lands are filled with ice and snow.
So, in the end, do they have a voice?
Whether it rains or snows,
they have no choice.
Deceived they are to think they're free,
while chains drag them on towards a destiny.
They be tall, they be small, they could die young after all.
These decisions are beyond their hands.
An untrusting creator puts in his demand.
And the joke is being free.
As free as the sea will let you be,
Is not that free to me.
The night will conquer every day.
In their deaths, they turn to clay.
And rise again to be led astray.
FOR WE ARE FREE, UNLIKE THEY.
Therefore,
freedom is such a fruitless way…wouldn't ya say?"
After minutes of prancing around and singing,
At the flick of his wrist, he threw me towards the ceiling.
And with the shake of his other hand,
the ceiling opened; I was high over all the land.

"Listen closely now, my friend.
A chance I give to end your end.
As you ascend towards the sky,
feel their laugh, feel their cry.
The orcs, the raiders, the souls of lost
toil in this world, but at what cost?
But if you do for me this thing,
I'll hand you my powers and make you, their king!
Ascend and rise, ascend and rise.
What could contain you, if not even the skies?
And forever you will rule this air,
whether they rejoice or live in despair.
It's up to you – will you do this thing?
Crush your destiny and BECOME KING!
The choice is yours; the choice is yours,
That's true freedom, baby, when the choice is yours."
As I'm perched high above all the world
like Ziyol sang,
I could see it all.
I could see them rise, could see them fall.
I could get used to this; it's true.
Sit here and enjoying the meadow rue.
Without a worry, without a care,
ruling over it all from mid-air.
What is the challenge, I wonder now?
It must be hefty for Ziyol to allow,
me to take his place, and rule in his stead,
for my decisions, he might dread.
And now I open up my eyes,
finding I'm still in bed.
"You have until sundown to make your choice."
Ziyol departs emotionless.
The myst now covers my trap.

15: Ziyol's Challenge Part 1

"On his knees before you,
bows a sinister man, whose done sinister things.
Made some sinister plans,
which now calls for a ruling.
Should he die by your command?
Should it be done by your hand?
Perhaps we throw him in the sinking sand,
or drown him in some barren land?
One thing's for sure; he does not fear,
the prison gates that hold him here.
Because of this, he must go.
Can we trust a prisoner
who doesn't truly show,
remorse for his crimes of past?
After all, would his repent last?
Hard to say – can't know for sure.
I swiftly recommend we close the door
on his days of roaming flesh.
And let him feel the ancient thresh
of the gods that once stood still,
And savored man's biting screams before their kill.
Tell me how, the morning snow pours.
Tell me now; the choice is yours.
All is yours as I sing.
Do this thing, and you'll be king!
Do this thing, and you'll be king!
Do this thing, and you'll be king!"
There was silence.
All the raiders, orcs, and humans

both free and bound,
stared at me, the prisoner and Ziyol.
"I confess to all that Ziyol sang.
Perhaps, I do deserve to hang
or be confined to some device,
that takes my bones to crush them thrice.
I'm full of guilt. I'm guilty of guilt.
And nothing can stop you from doing as thou wilt.
If I could do it all again, I'd do it all again.
I've murdered the innocent for payment.
I've deceived the innocent for payment.
I've stolen from the innocent for payment.
I've spent it all, and the debt is due.
But before you choose how I go,
a list of things I think you should know.
The being, Ziyol, who'll make you king
paid me off to do those things.
And look how the surrounding masses dread,
In Ziyol's haste, he wants me dead."
The man bowed humbly.
All I could see was his black clothes,
and a string of teeth around his neck.
Emotionless again, Ziyol stood
as if he knew what my choice would be.
I looked at Ziyol and looked at the man.
What I just could not understand
with all this blood upon his hands,
Why does Ziyol need me to make the demand?
Ziyol turned his back, head down, and walked away.
Hands clasped behind him.
His fingers motioned at the man in chains
and dragged him back to his cell.

Blood splattered from the man
as he was dragged along the spiked thorn pathway.
Aghh! Agh! AGH!
He screeched in pain.
Down to the pit of chains was he tossed.
Ziyol motioned towards a cage of rabid raccoons to head
towards the man.
At least twenty of them eagerly jumped him,
while the chains from the pit gripped him tightly.
He screamed.
I never heard such a thing.
Hours later, the sun gave way to the moon.
Still, he screamed.

16: Ziyol's Challenge Part 2

It was morning.
The next morning.
Raiders, orcs, and human prisoners going about
as if the previous day hadn't happened.
Not a cloud in the sky
though indeed, a chill engulfed the air.
Certainly, one of the more pleasant looking
days since I've been here.
I can't help but hear those screams from yesterday's prisoner.
I haven't been able to sleep.
He must be dead by now.
Death by raccoon? That's new.
"Perhaps you'd like to visit our guest?"
Ziyol shouted from the top of the prison stairs.
"Yes, I would certainly like to see how he looks, don't you?
I know deep down you do, Newcomer.
Just the mere thought has piqued your curiosity."
He ascended into the air above the stairs.
Oddly, he seemed in a joyous mood.
"Come, Newcomer. Come and see if raccoons are as hesitant
to deal out justice as you."
Uncontrollably, like a magnet, I was pulled off the ground.
I, too, was in the air, floating towards the prison pit.
"This would have been so much easier if you just would have
done the thing to be king.
Your hesitancy, sentiment, compassion,
whatever you call it, has cheated you out of greatness.
Why hesitate to be great?"
For the first time, I sense a kindness, if possible, in Ziyol.

We both descended while approaching the pit's edge.
The horror.
The horror.
The horror!
"Look at him, Newcomer, there slouched, in the corner, do
you see?"
How could I not?
"Your hesitancy of compassion brought him to this place.
Would it not be better if he weren't breathing?
If his right eye wasn't dangling from the socket like a
slink toy?
Blood drools from his mouth like a fountain,
while his flesh and garments are torn,
intertwined several times over.
You could have saved him.
It would've cost you nothing.
There he sits, slouched; life has ended, but still, he is not dead.
His body virtually torn apart, and clearly, he is only passed
out from pain.
Look at the hole in his ribs!
You did this.
He lives, yet maggots are already taking up residency
within him.
This is his soul turned inside out.
A wretched man who has done wretched deeds.
Barely alive, buried in his own urine, feces, and blood.
Do you still have compassion for him? Even now?"
I don't care about his crimes.
Seeing anyone like this is an absolute horror.
No one should suffer as he has.
Should they? I wonder.
I can't help but stare into his lifelessness.

He couldn't die soon enough. It would be merciful, I think.
"Then be merciful, Newcomer.
Do this thing, and you'll be king.
Stretch out your arm towards him and wish him ended.
It's a kindness, a mercy.
Do this thing, and you'll be king!
He won't feel or cause pain ever again.
Quite a win-win, wouldn't ya think?
He will sleep for hours and awaken in a horror state.
Full of pain, deformity, filth, embarrassment on
public display.
Should he? Should even he not be worthy to die in peace?
End it for him. Be merciful.
Do this thing, and you'll be king.
Do it!"
And still, I cannot bring myself to harm him.
He's done nothing to me.
I know nothing of his deeds beyond what's been told to me.
Ziyol, again emotionless, turns his back from me.
His hands clasped behind his back as he walks away towards
his palace.
His clasped fingers motion towards the many icicles hanging
from the massive black gates
They drop and fly towards the man, the prisoner.
All of them, nine, very pointy and sharp. Each about
ten inches.
Agh agh agh agh!!!
They pierce the man.
One in his left shin.
One in his right shin.
One in his left arm.
Two in each side of his groin.

Another scream, louder than the last.
Indeed, he is awake.
A larger one flew right through his now abandoned
eye socket.
Before he could pull it out,
His left and his right hands slammed behind him and nailed
him to the icy wall.
Where his ribs are exposed, another jolted him there.
"KILL ME!" he said in a whispery shout.
"You did this." Ziyol whispered into my mind.

17: Ziyol's Challenge Part 3

Have I slept at all?

The sun is rising.

I'm not in the plush warm confines of chambers given to me.

On the edge of the prison pits, I am.

My body is frozen, teeth chattering.

But…

I don't remember how I got here.

The last thing I remember was the ice piercing into
the prisoner.

Unless I am dreaming – he isn't there.

He's gone.

Not a trace of him remains.

How long was I asleep for? Days, weeks?

No way would that amount of blood and filth be scrubbed
away in mere hours.

"And yet…He's still…gone." Ziyol snickers.

Another morning, another strangely gleeful Ziyol.

"Mere minutes, actually, if your curiosity is diverting
your attention."

Indeed, it was.

"As I suspected.

Come now; time is not on our side.

Well, not on yours if current trends continue.

In the entranceway, there is one I'd like you to meet.

No, you won't be dealing with old Horatio,

Yes, that was his name.

That time has passed,

On to something more.

Come now.

Come follow.
Come see."
No floating this time.
We walked.
Ziyol put his left hand around my shoulder, grinning ear
to ear.
Literally.
"I was once like you, if you can believe."
I can't.
"I longed for things like Spring, and love, and happiness.
When those things eluded me, and I saw how well they wore
on others.
I became angry inside at myself.
I was angry at the world.
It made me cold.
I always felt like I was created to be special.
I was created to be adored.
Yet, the only adoration I received was that
which was taken by force.
Or deception, or meanness.
I had to accept that the coldness within would soon take over
my being.
It's who I was. It wasn't who I was meant to be but rather
who I became.
Without it – I would not be here,
as a god over millions in this palace.
I would NOT be ZIYOL, King of the Winterworlds.
I would probably be Lou, stocking the shelves in some earth-
bonded store.
Choice is powerful. It made me powerful.
Destiny makes us slaves.
Ziyol, who I am now, would crush Lou.

And you? Do you wish to stay as you are Newcomer?"
I know all those feelings.
I felt them and feel them.
Not a day goes by without them.
Others were born with so much.
And me?
Forgotten.
Left out.
Abandoned.
A misfit.
All my life. Desolate.
Now I'm an old man with nothing to live for but a glimpse
of what maybe could have been.
My life was turning around for the better.
I was closing in on Spring.
I know I was.
Until…
Until…
I don't believe it!
"THERE, Newcomer! Look at her! Look!
Groveling at the entrance of YOUR future palace.
Look at her! The wicked harlot.
The deceiver.
The defiler.
The destroyer of dreams.
Humbled before me – and YOU, should that be your wish."
H-How could this be?
"The mighty Princess Audience!
She sent orc troopers to follow you.
We killed them.
One.
By.

One.
Then we went to her meager orc barn and burned them
all alive.
Because of what they did to you-our future king.
Look at her! Pitiful. Her hair no longer vibrant,
now made of rust.
Her gown ragged, fangs dulled, and skin deformed.
What made her a ruler is a thing of the past.
Here, she seeks mercy and asylum.
Does she deserve it?
She knew of your dreams with the silhouette."
I give away my thoughts with an edgy look towards Ziyol.
"Oh yes, I know.
I know what she took from you.
But it's even more important that you admit it.
That you know she took it from you.
And then tossed you on the roof to take from others.
Her little orc babies, none yours mind you, are gone.
Not burned by us, no, we wouldn't dare-Khrimsonites we are
not.
But eaten by her.
Yes, in her orc appetite, she packed them for her journey,
And ate them all.
DENY IT, PRINCESS AUD, DENY IT!"
To my shock, there she was.
The Princess who shamed, used, and embarrassed me,
simply because she could.
The one who took my dignity and destroyed my destiny.
Her riches, which pale in comparison to Ziyol, flaunted in
my face.
She used my compassion for the Raider girl against me.

Maneuvered me to choose between a desired path and
her life.
Before Ziyol, she bows – sobbing.
"Here before us bows a murderer,
an adulteress, who never had to make a living.
She had every advantage and for the simple joy of it,
destroyed countless.
Without question, she brought her wrath upon you.
And when the riches were no longer satisfactory
she ate her young, not willing to go hungry for a few days.
After all, you did it, Newcomer.
You starved on your journey here.
Not her. Not her at all."
Ziyol was right.
"I DON'T DENY IT!" She wept and screamed!
"MERCY, I PLEAD!"
"Mercy? Newcomer, does she deserve mercy?
Do.
This.
Thing.
And.
You'll.
Be.
King!
Surely, this is a gift to you, is it not?
You've dreamed of taking revenge and justice upon
this Princess.
You've even WONDERED how you could pull it off.
And here she lies at our feet.
Being rid of an evil so pure…
How much better would the world be?
How much better would you be?

Knowing you righted such a wrong.
Would you believe that she wronged me once?"
Princess Aud looked upon Ziyol with wide eyes
Full of tears as if pleading with him to stop speaking.
"Oh yes. She wedded me once as well. Many years ago.
What a deceptress she is.
In fact! Newcomer, if you do this thing,
not only will you be king, but I,
even I Ziyol the great, will worship you.
None shall be greater in all Winterworld.
Stretch out your arm, friend. And all will be well."
Unlike the previous two days, my arm instinctively
stretched forward.

18: King's Order

On her knees, now facing me,
Princess Audience sobs.
I can't but remember the many flowing colors in her gowns.
Now she is covered in ash,
begging for mercy in the presence of many before me.
"N…newcomer. I've wronged you," she whispered.
"I used you and hurt you. I deceived you.
Yes. I plead for mercy. Please! I deserve death, but please!"
Since I first was hit by her deception in the Orclands,
I imagined many ways of ending her.
Now that time is here.
If I don't do this, for certain, a part of me will regret it.
Aud cannot be allowed to rule again.
My choices ruined my life. But hers brought me to a place
That kept me from destiny.
If I do this thing, I will be king.
She will be dead.
Can I live with that?
Can I live with achieving power,
through an enemy's death?
She deserves this.
I can rule and put things right.
I would not be like her or Ziyol.
There is an anger within me that rages in her very presence.
I didn't love her but married still at her request,
Her blackmail for another's life.
She used me and cheated me and others.
My heart is devastated seeing her.
Unwavering emotions are flooding my spirit.

I want to vomit.
"Good, this is good Newcomer. How transparent your hatred is."
Ziyol is gleeful.
"She wronged many. And how poetic that one of them
finish her."
I want to do this.
Not because I would be king.
That truly is a byproduct.
I want to end the wasted time and memory of her entirely.
Would killing her do that?
Could it bring the moments I've lost back?
Or will I be full of regret and her memories,
occupying even more of my thoughts?
Will killing her lead me to the silhouette?
Her death can't bring me to Spring, can it?
"Still thinking of Spring when you could be king?"
An annoyed Ziyol interjects.
"What can Spring offer you?
You, who are worthless to the world. And I am handing it
to you."
Something within me knows it isn't this simple.
I'm not a murderer.
Maybe in my thoughts, maybe in my pain, but it's not who I am.
Not who I want to be regardless of rewards or price.
I lower my arm.
"Well then. Can't say I'm surprised.
You are a failure for a reason." Ziyol snorts.
"BANISHED YOU ARE NOW! FROM MY SIGHT AND KINGDOM!
You are in the southernmost part of the world and eons from
your precious Spring."
Instantly my feet leave the ground with great force.
Ziyol throws me from the gate.

"Take your journey to Spring," Ziyol mocks.
"Because I am merciful, I will give you help even now.
Take the Princess and the bounty hunter
Whose lives you spared. May they aid you on your journey.
You will truly see what mercy is worth.
I ORDER YOU BANISHED – THE THREE OF YOU!"
BAM!
I hit the ground.
Shaken.
Two other thumps shake the ground near me.
Undoubtedly my two new companions.
To my shock, the city disappears as if it never was.
What have I done?

19: A Million Miles Apart

It's snowing again. Blizzard winds of great force push against
my every step.
Hot ice chips pelting my face like razors.
Nearly a day since the kingdom banishment.
No words have been spoken.
Not from me to the Princess.
Nor the Princess to the prisoner, Horatio.
Yet they follow close behind.
It is cold. Freezing cold.
It is yet hot. Blazing hot.
Frozen snow and burning ice pummel us with each step.
Loud, the winds are.
I don't think I would hear my companions even if they
were talking.
Several times, my own blood has splattered from my face,
only to be resealed by heat and ice,
and only to be re-opened again.
My senses have become so used to pain that it's
barely recognizable.
I look back to see both the prisoner and the Princess shielding
their faces.
Horatio stumbles with each step.
How he is still walking after the torment Ziyol placed upon
him is shocking.
I hear a melody sung through the wind.
It's a familiar one.
"Do this thing, and you'll be king,
Do this thing, and YOU'LL BE MY KING!"
Indeed, my ears aren't deceiving me.

In anger, the Princess is clearly mocking me.
Screaming at the top of her lungs so that she can be heard
by anyone through the wind.
"Why would he pick you? What an idiot! A fool!" She shouts.
I ignore, but once she gets started, there is no stopping her.
"That's probably why he chose you- because you are a fool.
He knew you wouldn't take the crown.
He had to know.
You could have killed the prisoner and saved us both?
We could be in a warm palace being served by now!"
Horatio shakes his head and continues onward.
"You know what I would have done, Newcomer?" she asked.
"I would have slaughtered both of you for the chance to be
king.
There… I said it. I will not apologize for it either."
Horatio, in annoyance, interjects,
"I don't need to be promised a throne to kill you, your
highness.
I'll gut you right where you stand…
For fun and for peace and quiet."
"NO ONE TALKS TO ME THAT WAY!
NEWCOMER TEACH HIM A LESSON!" Princess Aud shouts.
"No one is out here, your highness," the prisoner snaps back.
"It's just you, me, and the ex of yours who saved your life,
for which you are ungrateful."
I wonder how long all of this will last.
It's been a day only and a long one at that.

20: Praying for Pain

"I can't believe you have the audacity to call me that!"
The Princess shouts.
"Are you not that?" Horatio asks.
"Several hundred husbands, you have had? No?
And without divorcements?"
"How dare you?" Aud challenges back.
"You, who murder, steal and lie for profit mean to lecture me?"
"Everything you just said is correct." the prisoner answered
while sharpening a razor out of ice.
"I deny none of it."
"Well.. well.. umm.." the Princess murmurs.
She looks around as the winds temporarily calm.
"Newcomer, are…are you just going to let this…this thing talk to
me in that manner?"
"This thing has a name," the prisoner answers.
How in the world am I going to survive with these two?
The Princess pouted. "Who cares about your name!"
"Horatio," he answers. "Lasa Tio, they used to call me."
"I can think of other names to call you." Aud pouts more.
"Call me whatever ya like. As I said, it will most expectedly be true.
I deserved all of it, along with the wounds.
I have suffered for my crimes." He acknowledged while still working
on a razor.
"AGH AGH AGHHHHHHHHHHHHHHHHHHH!" Aud shouts in anger
and frustration.
"YOU ARE JUST SO INFURIATING!"
Evidently, Audience is incensed.
She sprints towards the prisoner screaming unknowable words.
She lunges for one of the razors Tio has sharpened
Now on his belt. With great speed,

the Princess secures a razor and then
in anger, stabs him in his shoulder.
Stunned, I am.
What just happened?
"AGHHHH That's what you get!" She shouts.
My jaw drops.
I move quickly towards Horatio to see if he is okay.
He looks down towards his shoulder, raises his eyebrows.
"Hm. You done yet?"
Blood is barely noticeable; it has frozen already.
"I feel nothing, ya know," Tio says back to her.
"So, stab away."
Audience quickly grabs another of his razors
And stabs him in the ribs.
SPLAT!
Before she could reach his ribs, Tio stabs Audience in
her chest.
Shocked she is. She freezes, dropping the razor.
A few seconds pass.
Silence.
The first silence I have heard in days.
"Ha!" Audience laughed. "Hahahahahahaha! I feel
nothing either!"
I always knew she was heartless.
To witness it with my own eyes...
"We are in the Yeldubs," Tio says.
"We feel nothing while we travel through it. It is of
great terror."
"Terror? To feel no pain isn't terror; it is bliss!" the
Princess retorts.
"You'd think so. But you will pray to feel it before the end. We
all will."

21: Dark Mirror in Remembrance

Alone in my thoughts, I am, in the after night.
I remember the end of my first week as Ziyol's captive.
Recalling my thoughts that one night.
I've committed murder.
How could I have known?
Yet somehow, I still knew what I was doing.
They deserved it, didn't they?
The Khrimsonites.
Destroying them saved lives, didn't it?
That room, so very different from the hospitality of the orcs.
The floating clear crystals above me were more magical
than the wooden planks over me in the orc barn.
The splendid size of my chambers far outweighed
the miniature-like rooftop where I was stationed.
Yet, it was far scarier.
Like a haunted child's dream.
I just knew there was a ghost around every pillar,
and behind each shadow within the corners of the room.
Indeed, there had to be a closet monster in such a place.
My fears, at an all-time high, and my heart felt faint,
when not pounding a bass drum out of my chest.
I heard Ziyol's "fairly well" over and over in my head.
The myst crept up to my right shoulder.
**I shuddered to think the possibilities should it cover
my body.**
Maybe I'm not evil, maybe an antihero.
Like a cool vigilante from the comics.
Oh, how I longed to be a child again reading those.
But I'm old at this point and dead inside.
I felt powerfulness and futureless, a sardonic cruelty.

The crystals, I recall, continued to seductively move about
the ceiling.
Were they watching me, I wondered?
I heard a low wind blow through the crystals.
One that sounded like wind chimes.
I heard them say something.
I heard them say, "We watch."
No No No No NO!
It's Winter, and it's windy.
I was in a scary place, and my mind was playing tricks on me.
I tried to convince myself.
Another breeze came through again.
"No tricks we watch," heard again from the windchime whispers.
"We watch for you to sleep."
Indeed, they spoke.
Why do they want me to sleep? I whispered in my thoughts.
Frightened, I continued to be.
Would I perish upon closing my eyes?
"You must sleep to see yourself," they answered.
They were apparently skilled at reading minds as well.
"Sleeeeeeeeeeep Newcomer-sleeeeeeeeeep."
 Their sounds were soothing enough to cause confidence in rest.
"You will be safe. We watch. And then you witness the reflection."
Not sure that was supposed to comfort me, and yet it had.
If it weren't for the moonlight beams entering the room,
that place would've been in utter darkness.
The winds continued to chime the crystals.
I tried to fight it.
With all my might I tried and still the more I fought, the sleepier
I became.
Before I completely dozed off, however
from all directions, the crystals began to meld together as one.
The soothing chime sounds were gone.

The ceiling above me became as a river,
with a stone recently dropped in it.
No longer were the crystals colliding, but ripples of water occurred.
I could see reflections of the incredibly large bed,
black reptilian blankets,
I was lying on.
I could see the moonlight beams in reverse.
And I saw a being.
It moved when I moved, and still when I was still.
In complete unison.
Sat up, lied down, raised left arm or right,
It didn't matter; it equal to my reflection,
except I could not recognize the face.
The Black Myst was also NOT in the reflection.
I looked at my own arm, and sure enough:
It was gone.
The water ceiling, slowed, got lower and lower,
which allowed me to see the reflection clearer and clearer.
The being was not me, but I knew it.
I'I saw this face before.
Glossy obsidian from head to toe.
It matched everything I did.
It was even my size.
I remember it getting closer.
It stared dead at me, or was I staring dead at it?
Still unsure.
It couldn't be more than ten feet above me.
I attempted to roll off the bed, but it was nearly as big as the ceiling
It was five feet away and then.
      four,
      three,
      two…
Stopped.

Face to face with this obsidian reflection of mine, I was.
I moved my left arm slowly to touch the water,
To see if it was real.
I felt no liquid, but indeed, it rippled at the touch.
My counterpart did the same as I did.
I then lifted my head and moved my face into the water.
A strange occurrence indeed.
I no longer saw the reflection.
I saw my borrowed bed from the ceiling view.
I saw what my counterpart would see.
Immediately I pulled my head back out of the water.
On the bed, as I was, and saw my counterpart again.
I couldn't help but stare at it some more.
And even though it matched my every move, there was
something unusual in all of it.
There was mystique in its personality.
"And how would you know that about me?" it said in many voices.
"How would you know I have any mystique at all?
I never spoke - not even once to you."
Confused and stunned.
I didn't expect this reflection to speak.
"You know me, don't you? Can you place it yet?"
It's true; I had seen this being before.
Quite recently, I knew it.
Agh, even still, I just can't place it at all.
In that moment, the water disappeared, and the crystals returned.
"You have awakened," they chimed.
The reflection vanished, and the myst on my arm was if it had
never left.

22: Dead to Death

It is the following morning?
Have I woken already?
Dreaming of the past has me exhausted.
"Here! Just try it!" Audience says to me.
"Just take this blade and shove it into my lungs-or heart even.
Trust me.
It's the strangest thing ever."
I can do nothing more than stare at her.
Her countenance glows with such excitement.
I fear her, nonetheless.
Like a child about to be given the sweetest of treats,
she pushes me on.
"You are such a bore, Newcomer."
She mocks.
"Tio has stabbed me eight times."
"Eight is an eternal number, mate," Tio exclaims.
"One more than perfection, which is only fitting for me." The
Princess responded
while transforming into a pure white lamb.
"Even greater than perfection, I am." She continued.
I wonder if she was a bully as a child.
Maybe she wasn't hugged enough?
SLAP!
Her right claw screeches across my left cheek.
I'm stunned.
My eyes water.
I can barely make a sound.
Yet I feel nothing.
"When I demand you do something, you do it, Newcomer!"

I stare in silence.
The dot on my arm, which had receded some since the exile,
grows instinctively for a moment.
I must exercise self-control.
I must not give in.
Audience grabs my left hand with both paws
placing an ice razor into it and then
forces me to jab her through her lungs.
I pull back in fear and panic. She drops to a knee.
"Ah!"
"Ah!"
"Ah ha ha ha ha ha ha!"
"Newcomer!" She rolls around on her back in laughter.
"This would have killed me in my Orclands."
My left arm is shaking. Instinctively, I backpedal away
from her.
BOOM!
I fall flat on my back.
"I should be dead!" she yells out.
"Even death is dead. I'm dead to death. Hahahahahahaha!"
Horatio's face changes suddenly from moderately amused
to complete horror.
"And yet, death still approaches."
Getting up, I whip my head around to see what caught his
gaze.
A mile from us, the ground erupts.
Snow, grass, dirt, water, and fire explode upward.
BAM!
On our backs we fall, as the ground shakes and shakes.
My eyes fix on the explosion.
From the ground, a long obsidian object rises up.
"Oh my…." Tio says. "RUN! RUN! RUN!"

He grabs Audience,
Who has not taken in what is approaching and pulls her up.
"RUN!" He shouts.
"What are you yammering ab…?"
She sees the object.
"It can't be."
For the first time I can remember, she is truly afraid.
Even more so than she was in Ziyol's presence.
"Klabuz!"
"Kla what?" Tio asks while slipping and falling from the
ground shake.
"Klabuz, the black scorpion of the deep.
One of the great titans."
She says this while falling with each step.
"We cannot escape."

23: Choice of Peril

Huff, wuff, puff, huff.
We all breathe and try to run from the beast.
"Keep moving, keep moving!"
Horatio shouts and pulls me up for the fifth time.
"Be in awe of its size after we escape."
"Don't you know what this thing is?" Audience screams
through the blaring sounds of the ground quaking.
"This is the Titan of Termin. None can outrun it!"
Horatio's muscular tricep smacks into my chest.
"Stay down, old man." His panic ceases.
"Don't move." He holds his hand out, motioning us to stay put.
Tio pulls out an Ice Sword comprised of the razors he had been
creating.
"If this is a Titan of Termin, the only way to defeat it is to stand
our ground."
The quaking stops.
The massive scorpion, at least fifty times our size,
 freezes with its stinger pointed in our direction.
"Equiaaaah!" it screeches.
"Maybe it will turn back?" Audience questioned.
"Not likely," Tio answers.
"Unless your sorcery can turn you into a meerkat,
I suggest you get behind me, your highness."
It seems Horatio's comment injected an idea into Audience.
Immediately her ears and eyes darken,
a tail grows behind her,
fur covers her body in one motion.
"Bounty Hunter, will this do?" she asks.
"Unbelievable." He shakes his head.

"What about you, old man? Anything in your bag of tricks?"
He glances at me.
Audience chimes in.
"He has the Mark of Myst.
He wields a weapon more powerful than any."
"Well, then get to it." Tio said to me.
"We are going to need everything to defeat this thing."
"He won't use it!" Audience shouted. "Something about morals."
Horatio grabs me by my garment, trying to shake sense into me.
"Now is not the time for morals, mate.
The death of morals is staring us in the face."
"Equiaaaah!" The titan screeches.
Tio releases me and points his sword towards the titan.
Audience, in meerkat body,
concocts an ice ball with spinning triangle blades
Moving violently in her paws.
We all looked at each other.
"You in?" he asks.
"I'm in!" Audience shouts.
"And you?" He looks towards me.
I nodded in affirmation moving my stance to charge
With a keen eye on the myst mark.
"Alright!" He yells.
"It's now or never, kids – here we GO!"

24: Champion

All is quiet.
Even Aud is silenced by the titan.
As three, we are lined side by side to face this
great hindrance.
Every beat from my heart alarms louder and louder.
How much more can I take?
Is this the new normal?
The scorpion stares then shrieks loudly once more.
A beaten hunter, a failed Princess turned meerkat,
and an old man stands as prey.
I can barely imagine how this will turn out.
"Arrrrgh!!!" Tio screams and charges towards the scorpion.
He fires a razor towards the titan, and it shatters on impact.
Don't think the titan noticed.
Still, in his stubbornness, Horatio continues to charge.
He whips out the swords of razors.
The titan certainly notices that and violently swings in
Tio's direction.
BOOM!
Tio flies twenty yards and is separated from his sword.
In horror, I watch, seeing he can barely move.
In life, he was a murderer, and now he is a warrior we
needed to survive.
Audience looks at me.
"Will you defend me?" she asks.
I stand still in silence.
She shakes her head, runs towards the beast.
I close my eyes.
She has no weapons but charm and deception.

I don't think that is enough.
As much as I hated her, I can't help but pity her again.
I can't watch.
I also know I stand no chance against this thing
with my feeble body.
With eyes closed, I imagine what it will be like,
should she somehow defeat the beast.
Knowing her, she would stand still and, by chance,
The scorpion would shrink, shrivel, and bow at the
mighty meerkat.
Then it would run away.
Not throwing a punch or drawing a weapon,
 "Hahahaha!" she laughs.
"Are you seeing this?" she joyfully shouts.
As it was in my thoughts,
so it is.
"This thing has shrunk into the cutest wittle scorp,"
Audience mocked.
"I defeated a titan. I'm a champion! Wooohoooooo!" She
dances and sings.
Slow to get up, Tio's face is that of disbelief.
But he isn't staring at her.
He is staring at me.
My arm had been outstretched during my thoughts.
"Your face," he says. "Half is covered in the myst."
Upon hearing this, Audience prances and sings more.
"Nothing can stop us. Nothing can stop us."
"For the first time on this journey," Tio says, "I fear she
is right."

25: Invierno Sconfitto

"Imagine what we can do!" says Audience.
"You can move mountains with your thoughts,
I can transform into anything,
and this one -well.. he's kinda useful.. kinda."
"You're wasting your breath," Tio answers.
"The Newcomer is ashamed of power. He seeks to hide it."
Horatio is right, and even though his tone is disappointed,
he also fears this power.
"Why?" Audience asks.
"The world is big out there with many hiding places
from the horrors of our past.
Poor decisions.
The nightmares we all live.
Why shouldn't we have a second chance?"
She stares at me.
"I wronged you, and you still protected me.
Maybe the three of us were meant to make it.
Maybe we were meant to overcome our
own inflicted misfortunes.
This is our life! Not the past, not our dreams.
The now.
Embrace that,
and the powers given us to do so."
Do this thing, and you'll be king.
Hauntingly, I hear the wind whisper.
"Legend has it, that those consumed by the myst,
meet their death at the full," Tio says.
"I've not met one to bear the mark such as you.
You are right to fear it.
Nonetheless, her highness has a point.

There be mighty monsters on our way.
Evil can often destroy evil.”
Or breed it, I think with alarm.
We walk.
They talk.
Equals and friends.
Our bodies, our lives, ripped apart and re-scrambled
over and over.
Dreams on the sharp hooks of fading hopes.
The slightest breeze enough to shred them.
Maybe this is the true purpose of life.
Not the whims of a dream,
but Forgiveness, and friendship.
Can I forgive one that wronged me so
to truly say I’ve learned nothing?
Would that not be an accomplishment in itself?
I stop walking.
The Bounty Hunter and Princess,
a few steps ahead, pause also.
“Something wrong, Newcomer?” Tio asks.
I step thrice towards Audience.
“It has been a long time,” I say.
Stunned looks on their faces. The breezes stop, the birds
are silent.
“D-don’t think I have heard your voice before, sir.”
Horatio is startled.
“He was my husband,” Audience answers.
“Yes, I know one of many, but I, too, never heard a sound.”
I lift my left hand and continue to speak.
“Everything Ziyol said was true.
You deceived me.
Wounded me.

Stole my dreams from me.
Forced me to trade principles for one's life.
Basically, enslaved me.
But as we, us three,
have fought together,
argued amongst ourselves,
And survived together,
In my heart, I know it is right to do this thing."
I look around, seeing their faces
hanging onto every word on one of those faded hooks.
"Audience, even so,
I
Forgive
You."
At that moment, involuntarily, my body lets out a sigh
of relief.
A burden unknowingly
I had been carrying.
A pain was lifted,
so powerful that it forced me to my knees.
My body quivers.
I am dizzy, or the ground quakes.
"Aggghh!" I screamed.
There is a physical pain,
as if something peels a long scab off a wound.
"Agggh!" I scream more.
It was a good pain.
There is a freedom in this pain.
Coming out of a land,
where physical pain didn't exist;
This is something special.
Then, I see it.

A miracle!
The Black Myst is leaving my body,
crawling onto the snow like an army of ants.
I am free.
Ha-ha, I let out soft laughter.
Rolling on to my back
I smile, genuinely, for the first time in an age.
"Newcomer," Audience says softly.
"That was beautiful,
all except for one small detail."
Even now, she has a complaint, I think.
"I never wanted your forgiveness.
Only
Your
Power."
Fear quickly overcomes my joy.
I look at the snow where the myst was.
It is gone.
Had it returned to me?
Am I cursed?
"No, Newcomer," she says.
"Look here, now."
She opens her right fist, and indeed,
my worst fear has come true.
The mark is buried within her palm.
"Do this thing, and I'LL BE KING!" she shouts.
"No!" Tio screams.
Instantly she turns towards him
shattering his existence into a million pieces.
He is gone.
Dead.
"Now, like a cat and its prey

I will toy with you, Newcomer,
until your death."
I turn to run.
She stops me.
I try to fight.
But can only resist so much.
She is subtly pulling the flesh from my bones.
Like needles, hundreds of them stabbing in and out of every
part of me.
It is unbearable
Just as I am ready to die,
she wakes my senses anew to freshen the pain.
"You are a fool, Newcomer.
Killed me, you should have."
She turned me, with new power,
towards her face so I would see her.
The mark already consumes half of her body.
It will soon control her.
"I will be KING in all the South world.
Even Ziyol will worship me."
"Where is your silhouette?
Your Spring?
Your Hopes?
Your Dreams?
Your Lions?
What return have you for your kind heart?"
Thunder! The ground beneath us shakes.
More intense and louder with every passing breeze.
This is not nature,
nor a rescue.
Thousands of orcs have come to see their leader,
And I surmise to feed on me once more.

"Aud, Aud, Aud, Aud!"
They chant.
Had I killed her, where would I be?
Certainly, not mired in this mix of sleet and muddy grass.
My fingers clean mud from the grass just to see green.
I haven't seen this since the journey started.
What is special about this place, I wonder?
Has grass always been here?
"My servants, my brothers, my husbands!" Audience shouts.
"You may feast on our guest!"
"YEAAA ARGGHH YEAA!!!" They shout in unison.
"BUT!" she shouts again, holding up her hand with the mark.
"Very, very small portions.
We wouldn't want to waste the freshness, would we?
Should he enjoy the spoils of pain?"
Again, they cheered and darted towards me.
I close my eyes, resigned to death, I am.
"To all I have hurt, I say aloud,
Please forgive me. Forgive me for the wayward son,
Friend, brother, colleague, human I have been.
Please forgive me and accept my repentance."
The cheering turned to grunting.
They are close. Should be closer.
I open my eyes. There is a fog ahead closing in with
great speed.
Something is protruding from the haze.
Many things!
Many
Daggers!
Firing with intense velocity toward the orcs.
Audience looks around
seeing her numbers quickly dwindling.

The remaining orcs, in fear, are fleeing.
"Stay where you are, brothers!" she shouts.
Then she lifted her arm toward the sky.
From the fog she forms a twister.
A mighty storm!
Those, unseen in the fog
Can be heard screaming as the storm tears them apart.
They are flung to other parts of the world.
Her entire body is consumed by the mark.
Unrecognizable, she is.
"Continue the feast."
She demands of the remaining orcs.
They step slowly towards me, quieter.
Fear is certainly upon them.
"What have you to fear?
Have you not seen my power?" she screams.
The orc furthest from me, she pulls close
with her power, and crushes his throat until death.
"This is what happens to those that defy me.
Now, let us eat!"
I close my eyes again.
Suddenly I am falling.
Resigned to my death.
Perhaps endorphins are comforting me
at my enemy's banquet.
What lies ahead, who knows?
I will in a moment or two.

...

...

...

I feel no gnawing.
No stench of orcs.

It is cold but not freezing.
A slight drizzle falls upon me.
Am I dead?
"On the contrary, my dear boy."
A man's voice I hear.
I open my eyes.
There are two figures before me.
A man with a kingly robe and crown.
Next to him, a lion, with a mane white as blinding snow.
"W-where am I? Where are the orcs?"
The man picks up my hand and pulls me to a stand.
"If there are orcs here,
they are not looking to feast on you."
"Lijah, you are in the land of Spring, where I, Nicholas, am
King – welcome."
The lion lets out a roar.
"Here is Marzo. Marzo is always at the entrance of Spring."
Lijah.
I have not heard that name in years.
That was my name at birth.
My name as a soul.
I lost it in that cave.
I had forgotten so much.
Somewhere I forgot who I was.
I just defined myself by my mistakes.
"Where are Audience and the orcs that were feasting on me?"
Nicholas chuckles.
"I'd say they are scrambling about looking for you.
No doubt she is throwing a tantrum."
Marzo majestically nods.
What an incredible-looking beast.
"And the fog? The daggers? Was that you?" I ask.

"That was your Raider friend, always looking out for you.
Your forgiving and asking for forgiveness brought you here.
The power was with you always," The king said.
"Now, your new journey lies ahead, Lijah.
In the land of Spring."
I smile for a moment.
I made it to Spring.
"Who is the Raider girl? Why me?"
He looks at Marzo and back at me with the kindest,
sympathetic stare.
"Soon."
I know to trust him but still have concerns.
"What of the people in the Winter world?
Should we not return to help them?
Audience and the myst are vile." I say.
"That is someone else's journey," Nicholas responds.
"Yours was not to defeat her."
"Guess I succeeded?" I ask.
He places his hand on my shoulder, gently turns me
towards Marzo.
"You heard my voice and did well." The mighty cat said.
"***Endure and be found.***
That was your mission. You did succeed," he continued.
A peace like none before settled upon me.
I am truly free.
"And the next journey?" I ask.
Nicholas smiles, "The silhouette, of course.
She stands at the end of Spring, you know.
At the gate of the lamb."
Uncontrollably and involuntarily, I smile.
Can this be real?
Can this truly be happening?

"Now go enjoy our beautiful lands, cottages, and
towns of people just being good folk to one another.
Enjoy your rest before saddling up for the next season."
I looked towards the town,
The rose gardens,
and water-wells.
The music and songs arising from the people,
of all races,
and all backgrounds
with magnificent countenances.
An appreciation for life and this world is etched in laughter.
It is beautiful.
The sun shines brightly on this world.
From the looks of things,
even brighter on the path ahead.

Rest

the season of singing has come,
the cooing of doves is heard in our land.

Song of Songs 2:12